First U.S. edition 2015

Library of Congress Catalog Card Number 2013955945

ISBN 978-0-7636-7318-5

CCP 19 18 17 16 15 14
10 9 8 7 6 5 4 3 2 1

Printed in Shenzhen, Guangdong, China

This book was typeset in Aunt Mildred.
The illustrations were done in pencil and paint, and colored digitally.

Candlewick Press
99 Dover Street
Somerville, Massachusetts 02144

visit us at www.candlewick.com

OINKINGHAM TV

WITH SPECIAL THANKS TO
AUDREY, OUR ART DIRECTOR,
AND OUR EDITORS, MARIA
AND MANDY.

WORST
IN
SHOW

written by
William Bee

illustrated by
Kate Hindley

CANDLEWICK PRESS

This
is Albert.

And this is Albert's pet monster, Sidney.

Albert thinks Sidney is the best
pet monster in the world.

And today Albert is going to prove it.
Albert is entering
Sidney in . . .

TELEVISION
THEATER

NO
LITTERING

There are five rounds in
THE BEST PET MONSTER IN THE WORLD!
competition, and the pet monster
who receives the most points
overall wins.

B.P.M.I.T.W.

The judges clamber all over the monsters with their measuring devices, and the monsters puff themselves up to show off their BIG

colorful

h a i r y WARTS.

Goodness —
the SIZE!

The HAIRS!

The JUDGES!
One faints, and another
breaks out in a rash.

Sidney has done his best.

But Sidney, who has a bath every other day
with lots of soap and bubbles, hasn't got any warts —
just a few freckles.

GOODNESS,
the EMBARRASSMENT!
thinks Albert.

Still, it's only round one — and who wants a big HAIRY WARTY pet monster, anyway?

ROUND 2
HIGHEST HOVER

*E*verybody has moved outside to see how high the monsters can hover. The judges use hot-air balloons and very long tape measures to measure the monsters' hovering height. Goodness — the HEIGHT! The WIND!

50FT

30FT

7

THE BEST
IN TH
COMP

40FT.

OINKINGHAM TV

5

8

The JUDGES!
One faints, and another
floats away in her
untethered balloon.

MONSTER
ORLD!
ION

Sidney has done his best.

But Sidney is scared of heights.
So Sidney hovers very near the ground — so near the ground,
in fact, that his feet are still touching it.

**GOODNESS,
the EMBARRASSMENT!**
thinks Albert.

Still, it's only round two — and who wants a pet monster
hovering around all day, BUMPING into things, anyway?

ROUND 3
MOST PARASITES

Some of the pet monsters have so many parasites that the judges have had to ask the parasites to get off their monsters and line up to be counted.

Goodness — the NUMBERS!
The VARIETY!

The JUDGES!
One faints, and another
starts scratching
frantically!

ENTER HERE

NO JUMPING!

QUEUE THIS WAY

Sidney has done his best.

But Sidney only has two parasites — Stan and Ollie.
And since Stan and Ollie are just staying for a few days...
they are really tourists rather than parasites.

GOODNESS,
the EMBARRASSMENT!
thinks Albert.

Still, it's only round three — and who wants a
pet monster with hundreds of parasites hanging around,
causing all sorts of MISCHIEF, anyway?

The monsters position themselves, and on the count of three ... they all FART!

Goodness — the SMELL!

The NOISE!

FARTOMETER

SMELLY! ROTTEN!

STINKY! WHIFFY!

STENCHY! PERFUMEY?

70

The JUDGES!
One faints, and another
runs off, holding his nose!

Sidney has done his best.

But a diet of frosted cookies and cupcakes
means barely a whiff —
and a sugary whiff at that.

GOODNESS,
the EMBARRASSMENT!
thinks Albert.

Still, it's only round four — and who wants a big SMELLY
pet monster, anyway?

It's the final round.

ROUND 5
HOTTEST BREATH

There is chaos onstage!
The monsters take in great
big gulps of air and breathe
out great big bellows of fire!
One of the TV cameras
catches fire, and so
do the curtains!

Goodness —
the HEAT!

The SMOKE!

The JUDGES!
One faints, and another
runs away, holding
her hot bottom!

Sidney has done his best.

But he has only been able to warm up a party sausage
that Albert has put on a little fork.

GOODNESS,
the EMBARRASSMENT!
thinks Albert forlornly.

SILENCE
THE WINGS

FIRE

FIRE

Still, who wants their BOTTOM
set on fire, anyway?

After all the day's excitement, at last it's time for the prize giving!

Albert and Sidney wait in eager anticipation as the dignitaries hand out the trophies.

HAIRIEST WARTS

MOST PARASITES

HIGHEST HOVER

Best in Show

SMELLIEST FARTS

But as trophy after trophy is
presented to the other pet monsters,
it becomes apparent to Albert and Sidney that they are not
among the winners. GOODNESS, the EMBARRASSMENT!

But wait!

Albert and Sidney's names are being called out!
Are they winners after all?

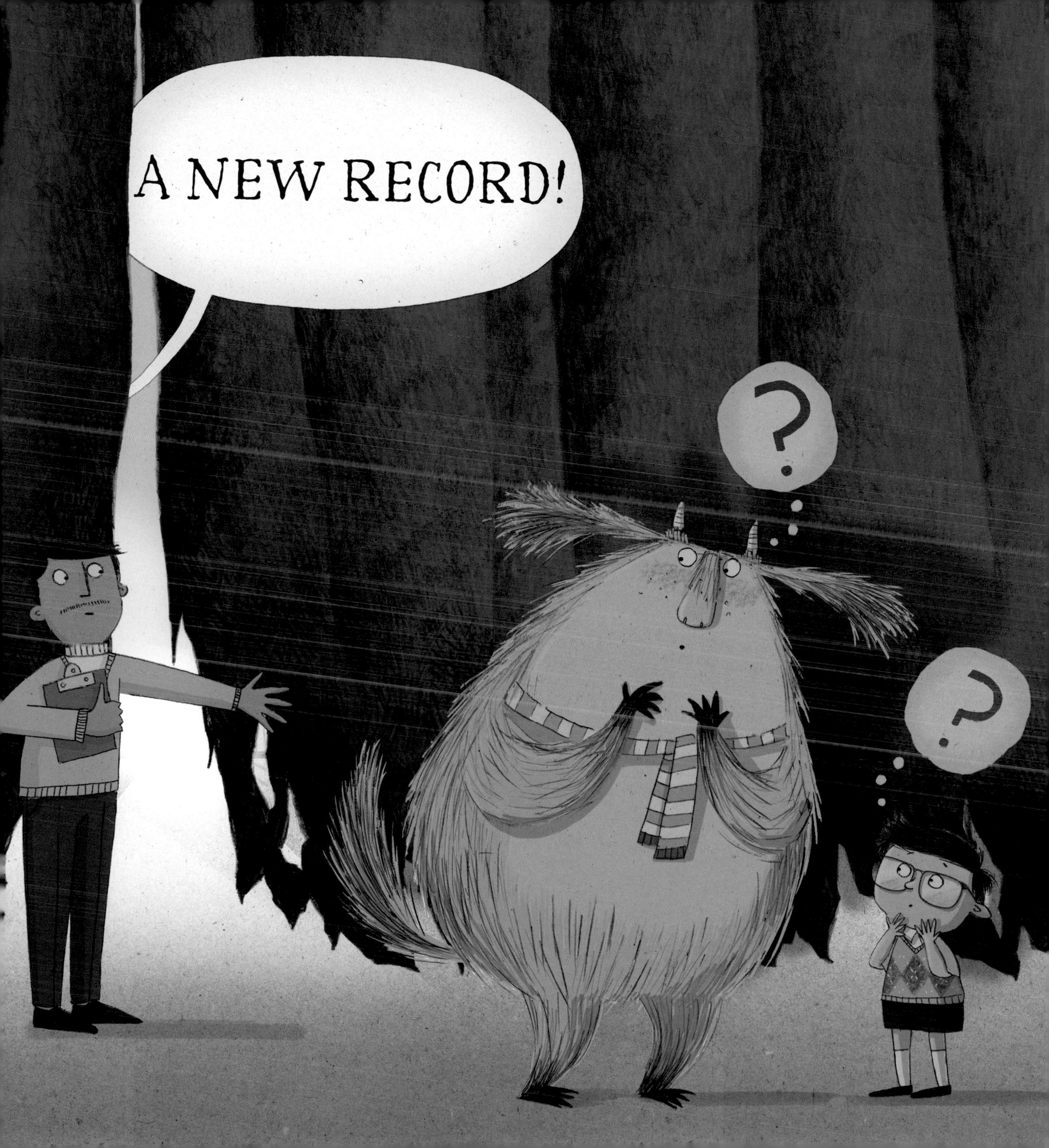
A NEW RECORD!
?
?

The lowest score in one hundred years! Freckles instead of warts! Zero for hovering! Two comical tourists instead of parasites! Pathetic sugary farts! And a lukewarm party sausage!

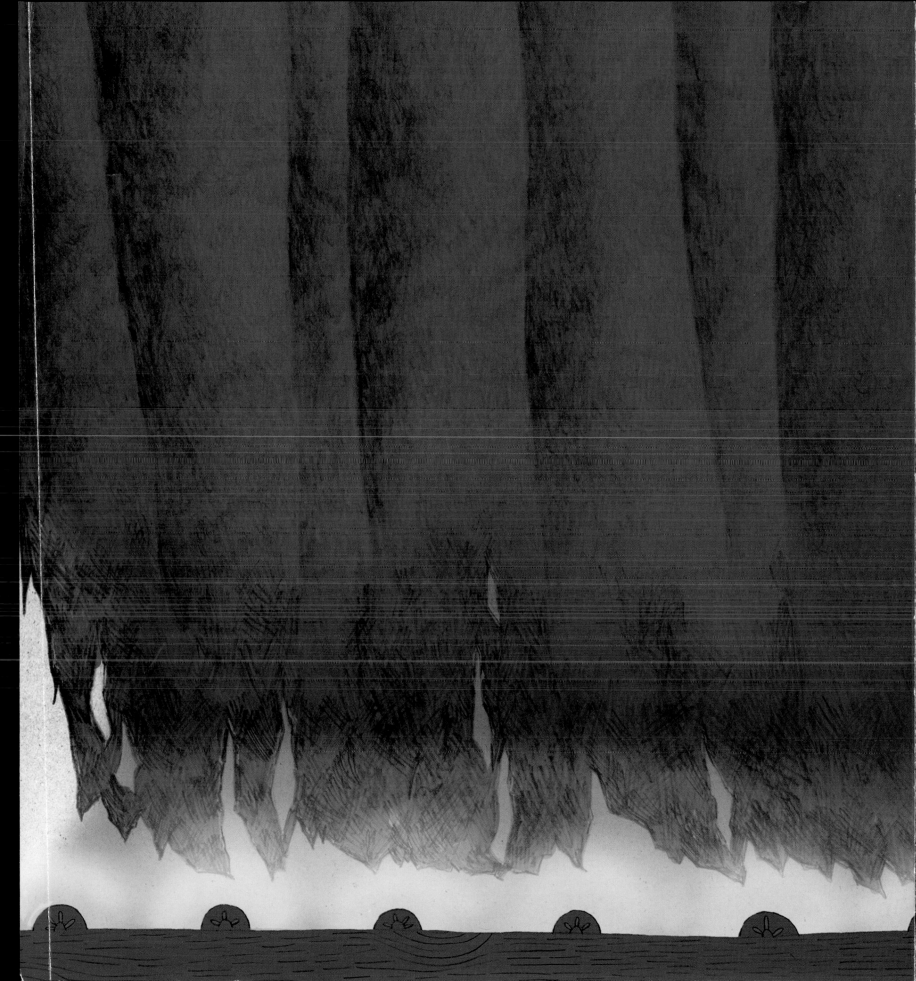

Worst in Show!

GOODNESS, the EMBARRASSMENT!
Still, thinks Albert, who wants a big HAIRY,
HIGH-FLYING, PARASITE-INFESTED,
SMELLY, FLAMMABLE
pet monster, ANYWAY?

SOLD OUT

B.P.M.I.T.W.

Especially when you can have a
BIG CUDDLY, LOVABLE . . .

BEST FRIEND.*

*(Who smells GREAT!)

HOME